HIGHWAY ROBBERY

Also by Kate Thompson:

The Switchers Trilogy:
Switchers
Midnight's Choice
Wild Blood
The Switchers Trilogy (3 in 1)

The Missing Link Trilogy:
The Missing Link
Only Human
Origins

The Beguilers (Irish Bisto Award 2002)
The Alchemist's Apprentice (Irish Bisto Award 2003)
Annan Water (Irish Bisto Award 2005)
The New Policeman (Guardian Fiction Prize 2005,
Whitbread Children's Book Award 2005 and Irish Bisto Award 2006)
The Fourth Horseman
The Last of the High Kings
Creature of the Night
The White Horse Trick
Wanted!

HIGHWAY ROBBERY

KATE THOMPSON

Illustrated by Jonny Duddle

RED FOX

HIGHWAY ROBBERY
A RED FOX BOOK 978 1 862 30515 1

First published in Great Britain by The Bodley Head,
An imprint of Random House Children's Books
A Random House Group Company

The Bodley Head edition published 2008
Red Fox edition published 2011

1 3 5 7 9 10 8 6 4 2

The Random House Group Limited supports The Forest Stewardship Council®
(FSC®), the leading international forest certification organisation. All our titles that are
printed on Greenpeace approved FSC® certified paper carry the FSC® logo. Our paper
procurement policy can be found at www.randomhouse.co.uk/environment

Set in Caslon Antique

Red Fox Books are published by Random House Children's Books,
61–63 Uxbridge Road, London W5 5SA

www.**kids**at**random**house.co.uk
www.**totallyrandombooks**.co.uk
www.**randomhouse**.co.uk

Addresses for companies within The Random House Group Limited can be found at:
www.randomhouse.co.uk/offices.htm

THE RANDOM HOUSE GROUP Limited Reg. No. 954009

A CIP catalogue record for this book is available from the British Library.

Printed and bound in Great Britain by CPI Bookmarque, Croydon, CR0 4TD

For my wonderful neighbours,
Peter and Ann

CHAPTER ONE

There are good things and bad things about being small. You wouldn't know about that, though, would you, sir? Fine tall gentleman like yourself. But it's true. One good thing is that people often mistake me for being much younger than I am, and that makes them take pity on me.

Especially the women, the ones that have their own children at home. And especially the poor ones, who know that there isn't much keeping their own little ones from begging in the streets like me. Not that I'm begging now, sir. I wouldn't want you to think that, not for a minute.

I had a change in my fortunes, sir, you see. You might not know it from looking at me – not yet, anyway. But it's true all the same. And if I hadn't been so small, it would never have happened.

You see, one of the bad things about being small is that most of the other beggar lads on the streets are bigger. And if you're bigger, you can throw your weight around, so to speak. You can choose the best place to beg and no one's going to bother you, provided you don't annoy the shopkeepers and scare off their custom. But if you're small, it's different. Whenever I found a good spot I was always chased off by some bigger lad, and many's the bruise I've had to show for it, you can take my word on that. One fellow hit me so hard I couldn't hear anything for a week.

But that was some time ago, sir, and I can hear as well as anyone now.

Why I'm telling you this is by way of explanation for how I ended up begging so far from the centre of the city. I was way out on the outskirts on the day my luck changed. It was a cold, miserable day that couldn't decide whether it wanted to rain or snow. I had a pair of boots once but they were so often wet that the nails came through and it was like trying to walk on a pair of hedgehogs, and that's the truth, sir. I let another lad steal them off me just for the pleasure of hearing him howl when he put them on.

But on that day, on the edge of the city, I had no boots and my feet were as cold as

ice and my hands were not much better. I
was hungry too, but then I'm used to that.
I do remember a time when I wasn't
hungry, sir, but it was only for a very short
time and it was a very long while ago.
There wasn't much traffic through that
street, either. It was one of those nasty,
muddy little streets, all pigs and gardyloo,
which carts avoid because they're always
getting stuck. There were a few people
walking, but no one who came along had

a coin or a crust of bread to spare for me, so all in all it looked as if it was going to be a very bad day for me. But then, in the blink of an eye, my luck changed.

I heard him before I saw him. I heard him through my stone-cold feet first, and then I heard him through the air, and he was like a distant storm approaching, so I couldn't tell what I was hearing. Then the sound grew nearer and clearer. It was galloping hooves, clattering through muck and ice.

Round the corner he came, a tall rider on a big black horse, and the pigs and chickens cleared the road in double-quick time to get out of his way. I stepped back myself, sir, even though I was already well out of the road, and I squeezed myself tight against the wall. Still he came on, at full tilt, his black cloak streaming in the air behind him, and now I could see his face, his cheeks red from the cold and his moustaches as black as the black horse under him.

He didn't look at me at all as he came on, but I saw his eye fix on something beside me. The alleyway, I think it was. And just as he drew level, he straightened in the saddle and reined in the mare so fast she sat

right down on her tail in a shower of mud. Some of it hit me in the face, sir. That's how close I was.

The rider sprang off as light as a cat and pulled the reins over the horse's head. Then he marched straight over to me and put them into my hand. I gaped up at him and my mouth must have been as big as a badger hole. You can imagine, I'm sure, how astonished I was. He was very tall, that man, and his cheeks were red and he was breathing hard and there were tear-tracks across his face. He looked wild and mad, sir, and I have to admit that the sight of him terrified me.

But of course, the way he looked was not because he was angry or excited but

because he had been travelling so fast
through the icy weather. And indeed, when
he opened his mouth, it was not to yell at
me, which is what I expected, but to say,
quite gently:

'Hold the mare for me, lad.
And when I come
back, I'll give
you a golden
guinea.'

And he
ruffled my hair
for me, sir. Look.
Like this. Made
it stand up like
a bunch of straw. I would have done
anything for him after that. I don't often

meet with kindness, as I'm sure you can imagine. So I clutched tight to those reins and I closed my badger-hole mouth and I nodded my head until my teeth rattled.

'You can rely on me, sir,' I said. 'I won't move an inch from here until you come back.'

'Good lad,' he said. He pulled a saddlebag from the horse's withers, then unfastened his cloak and laid it carefully over her back. That will tell you, sir, how much value he set on his mare, because it was a cold day for a gentleman to be out and about in his shirt-sleeves. He patted her on the neck, winked at me, and then he was gone, slipping away down the alley and out of sight.

CHAPTER TWO

𝕴 was as hungry as a sow with ten piglets, but I was full of satisfaction. I don't know if that makes sense, but sometimes a bit of kindness goes further than a meat pie. And to be trusted too. To be given a bit of responsibility. That can make you feel like a man even if you're only as high as a man's elbow.

And that horse, sir. I don't think I'd actually ever held one before that. Most horses I see are pulling carts and they don't need anyone to hold them. If the

driver gets down to make a delivery or
to go for a pint of ale, those carthorses
just wait there until he comes back. And
as for carriage horses, the footmen won't
let the likes of me anywhere near them. I
don't know why. Maybe they're afraid I'd
give them fleas or something. But there
I was, holding this horse, and she was
huge! Sixteen hands if she was an inch.
And so beautiful. Her nostrils were red as
cornfield poppies. Her eyes were wide and
bright with the excitement of the gallop
and she kept looking this way and that, as
though she was still seeing the countryside
speeding past.

I was, I have to admit, a little afraid
of her. She was so massive and hot, all

covered with mud and steaming like
a dragon that could burst into a fit of
violence at any moment. And she was very
restless to begin with because she had been
ridden so hard and so fast. In that way, I
suppose a horse is pretty much like a man.

They neither of them can shut down their feelings as quick as they'd like to. So the mare was looking from side to side and moving from foot to foot, and then she planted her four feet out wide and shook herself so hard that the saddle-flaps rattled and the black cloak slipped sideways.

But for all her restlessness she never once tried to break away from me. She didn't even pull on the reins. A pure-hearted lady through and through, sir, if ever there was one.

And as she calmed down, I became more confident, until finally I found the courage to reach up and run my fingers down the front of her nose. She let out an enormous sigh and dropped her head.

I could reach it better now and I stroked
her forehead and combed her black
forelock with my fingers. I swear she liked
it, and I wondered whether horses were
like boys, and whether they too felt the
need for a bit of kindness now and again.

So holding her was easy, but there was
something that made it better than easy
and turned it into a pleasure. The mare, as
you would expect, was blowing hard, and
her hot breath was coming straight at me
and warming my miserable hands and feet.
For a long time I just stood and soaked
up the heat, and gradually my stony hands
and feet came back to life.

But nothing lasts for ever. In time the
mare's breathing returned to normal, and

the cold made itself felt in my bones again. I began to wonder when the gentleman might be coming back and when I might be setting eyes on my golden guinea. I had never seen one before, and I tried to imagine what I might do with it. I thought about hot pies and pigs' trotters and apples and pease pudding. I thought about the marketplace where you could buy hand-me-down boots for a shilling and patched woollen blankets for sixpence. And I was thinking so hard about hot bread that I began to imagine I could smell it. And then I realized that I wasn't

imagining it, after all. I really *could* smell
it, and I could see it as well, in the hands of
two young girls who were walking along
the side of the road towards me.

CHAPTER THREE

What are you doing?' asked the taller of the two. She had a pigtail, and her grey skirt had a black band along the bottom where the hem had been let down.

'I'm holding this horse for a gentleman,' I said.

'What gentleman?' she said.

'A gentleman,' I said, 'who doesn't choose to give his name to little girls.'

'I'm bigger than you are,' she said.

This was true, but it was also irrelevant, so I didn't answer.

see a horse in a cloak before?'

Squint was right beside me now, reaching out timidly towards the mare's nose. I elbowed her aside.

'Look,' I said, 'if you're really so keen to touch Her Grace, it might be arranged. But it will cost you.'

A minute later I was cramming the first of the penny loaves into my mouth and the other one into the poacher's pocket titched inside my patched old coat. The two girls swarmed over the mare, oohing and aahing, stroking her nose and her eck, putting little plaits into her mane and tail, and doing a really good job of straightening the cloak on her back so that hung down exactly the same amount on

'Anyway,' she went on, 'there aren't any gentlemen around here.'

I didn't answer that, either. They stood and watched me. I watched the horse and didn't look at them, though I couldn't help stealing the occasional glance at their penny loaves. They had one each, and they were hardly even nibbled. I don't mind telling you, sir, the smell made me feel faint with hunger.

'Why is he wearing a coat?' said the smaller girl, after a while. She had a bad squint and I couldn't tell whether she was looking at me or at the horse. She might have been looking at both of us at the same time.

'It's not a he,' I said. 'And she's wearing a coat because she's the most valuable horse in England and she needs to be kept warm. When she's at home in her stable, she wears a felt bonnet and a silk gown, and she eats plum duff and oranges.'

Squint giggled. 'No she doesn't.'

'And figs,' I added. 'She's particular[ly] fond of figs.'

She was edging closer. If it hadn't b[een] for the horse, I could have snatched h[er] penny loaf and run for it. I came up w[ith] another way of getting it.

'In fact,' I said, 'this horse is so spe[cial] that it's costing me a shilling for ev[ery] hour I'm allowed to hold her.'

I stroked the mare's nose and she [gave] her head to me again.

'I don't believe you,' said Pigtai[l. 'I] heard of anyone paying just to ho[ld a] muddy old horse.'

'She may be muddy,' I said, 'b[ut that] doesn't mean she isn't special. D[on't]

each side. The mare was very patient with
all the attention, sir. I'd swear she knew
what was going on, because she arched
her neck and fluttered her eyelashes, and
with all the grooming she was getting
she actually began to look like royalty.
But after a while I could see that she was
starting to get restless, so as soon as I had
swallowed the last of my loaf I told the
girls that their time was up.

'If the master comes back and catches
you, we'll all get a good hiding,' I said.
'And you must swear on your mother's
grave that you won't tell anyone about
what you just bought.'

'Why?' said Pigtail.

'Because I shouldn't have let you,' I said.

'And if you tell other people, they'll all
want to come and hold Her Grace, and
then I'll have to fight them off, and the
master will come looking for you and he'll
put you in prison.'

The girls went off looking worried,
and I fingered the second penny loaf in
my pocket. To eat it or not to eat it, that
was my dilemma, sir. I doubt if it's one
you ever came up against. The thing is, if
I ate it, there was no more evidence, and
if the girls told tales, then it was their
word against mine. But if I ate it, then I
wouldn't have it to eat later, and there was
no telling how long it would be before my
gentleman came back. I decided to save it,
at least for the moment.

CHAPTER FOUR

The gentleman had been gone a long time by now, and I was beginning to be anxious for him to come back. I watched the pigs and chickens foraging around in the icy mud and wondered what they could possibly find to eat in that mess.

The street was empty for a while after the girls had gone away, and then a couple of farmers came along, driving some sheep to the butcher's, and then a man in a firewood wagon, which was making heavy weather of the mud, and then a washerwoman with a massive bundle tied up in a grimy sheet. They all looked at the horse and at me, but no one stopped or spoke. Soon after that, though, a man came along and he took a great interest in me and the horse. I saw him looking at us as he came along the street, and when he drew level, he stopped walking and stood looking.

I didn't like the cut of him, sir, from the time I first laid eyes upon him. When you

live on the street, you get to know a lot
about people. It's a question of survival.
And this man looked shifty to me. He
crossed to my side of the street, as I had
guessed he would, but for a long time he
didn't say a word. He just walked round
the horse, looking her up and down and
over and under and through and through.

'Who does it belong to?' he said at last.
He wasn't that old, but he'd already lost
most of his teeth and his speech wasn't all
that clear.

'None of your business,' I said.

He glared at me so hard that I feared he
might aim a blow at me. I knew it wouldn't
cost him a second thought. He was no
stranger to violence, that fellow.

'How much you asking for it?' he said.

Well, I don't mind telling you, sir, that
his question made me stop and think. It
hadn't really occurred to me before, despite
what I had said to the two girls, but that
mare was certainly worth a lot of money.

The man was watching me thinking,
and I wished I could come up with a smart

31

answer, but I was stuck fast in a conflict between the prospect of money and loyalty to the gentleman rider. How much was she worth? That was what I was thinking. An awful lot more than the guinea I'd been promised, that much was certain.

'You're tempted, aren't you?' He stepped closer to me as he said it, and glanced quickly up and down the street.

I wouldn't like you to get the wrong impression, sir. I might be poor but I'm not a thief. All I'm saying is that the prospect of a large amount of money couldn't be passed over without due consideration.

'Indeed I'm not,' I said, but I knew my words lacked conviction and I'm sure old Toothless knew it too.

'Hmm,' he said, and went about inspecting the mare all over again, though I very much doubt there was anything about her he hadn't seen on his first go round.

I looked at her too, with eyes wide open now and with numbers in my mind growing bigger and wilder by the moment. The kind of money the mare might fetch could lift a lad like me out of poverty, sir. Set me up in my own little business, perhaps. Selling pies or muffins around the markets. Or shining boots like yours, sir. I'm sure that you can understand why I was engaged in such a fierce battle with my conscience.

Old Toothless turned to observe a cart that was trundling slowly towards us, and I turned to look at it too. It was loaded with turnips and carrots and guarded by two burly farmers, one in front at the horse's head and the other sitting behind. Both of them carried cudgels.

When I turned back, Toothless had disappeared. There hadn't been time for him to get to the end of the street and I guessed he must have turned into one of the alleyways. My dreams of money had gone with him but I was glad that it was over, and that the dreadful temptation had been removed.

Chapter Five

The farmers stopped to admire the mare. They were both nearly as broad as they were tall, with bulging forearms and heavy shoulders.

One of them had a great head of hair like a haystack but none at all on his chin. The other was practically bald on top but had a gingery beard

which grew right down on to his chest.
It was so thick, a family of wrens might
have been nesting in it. I thought that if
you turned his head upside down, he would
probably look exactly like his friend.

'Ee, but she's a grand mare,' he said, and
gave her such a hefty slap on the neck I
was afraid she'd fall down.

Haystack gave her a pat on the rump.
'Who does she belong to, then?' he said.

You know, sir, it never occurred to
me for an instant to mistrust those two.
Maybe it was the slow, solid way they
moved, or the hard days of work stored
up in their muscles, or maybe it was just
their eyes, blue as the summer sky and
filled with nothing but wonderment.

So I told them about the gentleman and his wild ride into town, and I told them about the promise of the golden guinea, and I told them as well about old Toothless and his sneaky attempts to buy the mare.

'He was wasting his time there, wasn't he?' said Haystack. 'Good honest lad like you. He'd get nowhere with that game.'

That made me feel good, sir. It almost made me believe that I had never even considered old Toothless's proposition.

'Never trust a bloke like that, anyroad,' said Wrenbeard. 'Sure as not he'd have some sharp lad waiting round the next corner ready to rob the money straight back off you.'

Those farmers might have been slow,
but they certainly weren't as stupid as they
looked. I thought I knew every street trick
in the book, but I hadn't thought of that one.

They had a small barrel lashed to the
side of their wagon, and since they had
stopped, they took the opportunity to pour
a drink of water from it. They gave me a
dipper of it as well, which was welcome.
The mare grew very excited when she got
a scent of it.

'She's thirsty, God bless her,' said
Haystack. When you think of it, she was
bound to be, wasn't she, sir, after such a
long hard gallop. But it hadn't occurred to
me, being as how I'm so ignorant when it
comes to horses. There wasn't enough for

her in their little barrel, but they had a
bucket for their own horse, and Haystack
went off with it in search of a pump. When
he came back, the mare plunged her nose
in until her nostrils were completely under
the water.

'You don't often see that,' Wrenbeard
said. 'Most horses keep their nostrils
clear.'

'Sign of a great heart,' said Haystack.

'Is it?' I said.

'So they say,' said Haystack.

'So they say,' said his friend.

They were completely besotted with
her, sir, and very reluctant to move on.
Haystack fetched a second bucket of water
and Wrenbeard fed her carrots with the
tops on and a handful of the oats they
had brought for their own mare, though
it didn't please her one bit and they had
to give her some too. I wanted to keep
those two fellows with me for ever. They
were big and strong and gentle, and they

carried their slow, country ways with them wherever they went. Even when another cart came along behind them, they were in no hurry to leave, and it wasn't until the other driver got impatient and began to call them bad names that they eventually took their leave of the mare and me, and picked up their cudgels and went on their way.

Chapter Six

I missed them when they had gone and so did the mare. I swear it, sir. She whinnied after them, and it was the only time during the whole day that she made any kind of sound or took any kind of notice of anyone. But there was someone else who was only too pleased to see the back of those country men. Old Toothless. When I saw him coming back,

43

I had a feeling that he'd been there for
a while, waiting for them to move off,
hiding down one of those dark little alleys
like the gutter rat he was. This time he
had someone with him: a stout man in a
waistcoat and a pair of very muddy riding
breeches. You might think his attire
marked him as a gentleman, sir, but I assure
you he wasn't. He might have been better
dressed, but he was made of the same stuff
as Toothless, without a doubt.

And like Toothless had done, he never looked at me at all, but walked around the mare and examined her from every angle you can imagine. And when he'd done that, he strode up to her head, and without any warning or by-your-leave he pulled open her lips to look at her teeth. She didn't like that, sir, not one bit. She threw up her head and backed away into the road, and since I wasn't about to let go of her, she dragged me with her through the mud and the gardyloo.

I protested, sir. I asked them what they meant by assaulting my master's horse in such a way and told them to take themselves off, though not in such polite terms as that.

'Who is this master of yours, then?' the man in the waistcoat asked me. 'And why has he abandoned his horse in the middle of a pigsty?'

'He hasn't abandoned her,' I said. 'He has left her in my keeping. He's sure to return very shortly, and if you know what's good for you, you'll leave well alone, because if he were to catch you gawping into her mouth, he wouldn't take kindly to it.'

'But he can't think much of her, can he?' he said. 'To leave such a fine animal

standing in a muck sweat with nothing but
a guttersnipe to care for her?'

'I won't have you calling me a guttersnipe!' I said.

This sent both the men into gales of
laughter, and while they were occupied
with that I led the mare back to the side

of the street. She followed me like a lamb and I rubbed her nose for her so she would know I was pleased.

'I like this lad,' said Muddybreeches. 'Shall we let him in for a share?'

I don't think Toothless cared much for that idea, but he made no objection and the other one told me his plan.

'I buy and sell a great many horses, and I prefer my dealings to be above board. So I propose to give you thirty shillings for this mare.'

'Thirty shillings!' Toothless spat, but Breeches ignored him and continued like this:

'That way you won't go home to your gutter empty-handed, and I can say I bought the horse fair and square. I shall get perhaps seven guineas for her and my friend here will get a share for bringing the matter to my attention. So what do you think of that for an arrangement?'

Thirty shillings was tempting. It was, after all, a full nine shillings more than the guinea I had been promised. And it was all the more tempting when I saw the coin purse come out and heard the very fine jingling sound it made.

'He'll never find you again, lad,' said Toothless. 'Runt of a thing like you can lose yourself easily enough in a big city like this.'

I looked around the street and became aware of a new danger. The two carts had disappeared, leaving deep muddy troughs in their wake. The pigs were already in there, digging in the bottoms with their filthy snouts, but there were no people to be seen anywhere. What was to stop these two crooks from taking the horse anyway and leaving me with nothing? How could I stop them, after all? And that fine gentleman wasn't going to give me no guinea for losing his horse, was he? But still I couldn't agree to it. I was all

puffed up and full of my own virtue, after what those two farmers had said about me. Besides, I hadn't forgotten about that smart lad, who was probably waiting round the corner. I was resolved not to give up that horse without a fight.

'I won't let you have her,' I said. 'Not for thirty shillings and not if you were to offer me thirty guineas.'

I tightened my grip on the reins, gritted my teeth and got ready for the blows that I was certain would come next. But yet again the heavens smiled upon me. For the second time that day I felt thunder coming up through my feet, then heard the clatter of hooves approaching along the road, then the jingle of bridles, the delighted calls of

51

a young child round the corner, the squawk
of a chicken that moved too slowly. Then
they came thundering into view: a dozen of
the king's soldiers in all their finery. They
didn't come as fast as the gentleman on his
black horse had done, but it was clear that
they had been riding hard because their
horses were lathered with sweat and there
was so much steam rising from them that
it looked as if the soldiers had brought
their own cloud along with them, in case
they needed rain.

I pulled the mare closer in towards
the houses at the side of the street, to
give the soldiers more room to pass by,
and as I did so, I noticed that Toothless
and Muddybreeks had vanished just

as silently as the
confess I wishe
easily because.
street beggars
natural allies
couldn't pre
either. Al
to themse
They st
a horse
like a

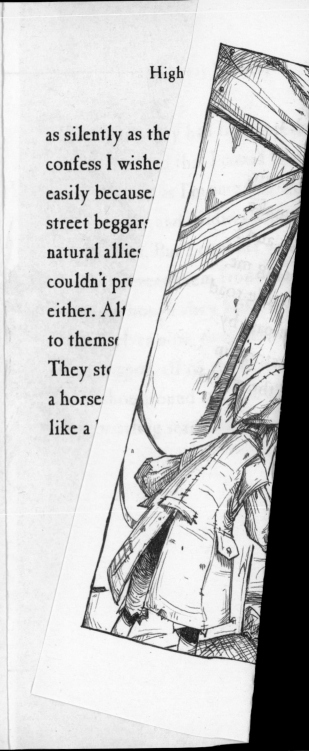

CHAPTER SEVEN

The black mare shifted restlessly and snatched at her bit, and it seemed to me that she was as anxious as I was. The soldiers' horses pawed the ground and tossed their heads impatiently. One of the soldiers got down and handed the reins of his horse to another.

'Whose horse is this?' he asked me.

I swear a dozen different answers jumped into my head, but since I couldn't decide which one to use I let them all get away again, and I said nothing at all. The soldier

bent down in front of me until his hard
grey eyes were level with mine.

'Do you speak English?' he asked, very
slowly.

I would have laughed if I hadn't been so
afraid.

'I do, sir,' I said.

'I do, Captain,' he said.

'I do, *Captain*,' I repeated.

'Whose horse is this?' he asked again.

'It belongs to a gentleman,' I said,
deciding that it was safest to be honest
about it. 'And he has promised me a guinea
if I hold her until he comes back.'

The captain straightened up and began
to walk round the mare in a very similar
manner to the two crooks. She gave a great

sigh, as if she was exhausted with being examined. The captain lifted her feet and peered at her shoes, then he looked at the cloak and at the saddle underneath it.

'She's not for sale, sir,' I said.

'*Captain*,' he corrected me.

'She's not for sale, Captain, sir,' I said.

'What a shame,' he said. 'She's a very fine animal.'

I was as proud to hear that as if she had been my own, and I found that, despite myself, I was beginning to like this soldier.

'She is indeed, Captain,' I said.

'But tell me more about her owner,' he said. 'What does he look like?'

'As tall as you, sir, Captain, sir. Or very

nearly. And he has big black moustaches and long, curly black hair.'

'I see,' said the captain. 'And was he carrying anything with him, do you remember?'

'A saddlebag, Captain. That's all, as far as I remember.'

'Good lad,' said the captain, and he ruffled my hair just the way the gentleman had done earlier, though I noticed that he wiped his hand on the leg of his breeches afterwards, and the gentleman hadn't done that.

He walked back to the scarlet fence and said something to another of the soldiers, and that one dismounted too, and they walked off together to a quiet place further down the road. They had to go

some distance, because quite a crowd had
gathered by then, and there was a second
horseshoe of curious onlookers crowding
round behind the soldiers. Everyone was
looking at me and it felt very pleasant,
sir, to have all those eyes upon me and
the fine black mare. It made me feel very
important.

But it wasn't to last for long. The captain soon came back and gave an order to his troop, and straight away the soldiers began to clear the crowd and send everyone off about their business. Then the soldiers too went away, leaving only the captain and the one he had been talking to, and the two horses belonging to them.

The captain came up to me and bent his knees again so he could look me in the eye.

'What's your name, boy?' he said.

I told him, and he went on, 'Well, it seems to me that you are a most trustworthy young man.'

I nodded earnestly. As I'm sure you can tell by now, sir, this was very perceptive of the captain.

'Good lad,' he went on. 'Good lad. And how would you like to do a piece of work for the King?'

'I should like that very much, Captain,' I said.

'Good,' he said. 'And you won't find it difficult at all.'

For a moment I dared to imagine myself dressed in scarlet uniform and riding the black mare into a fearsome battle- but it was not that kind of work that the captain had in mind.

'Have you ever heard of a fellow called Dick Turpin?' he asked me.

'Dick Turpin the highwayman?' I said.

'The very same.'

Of course I had. Who hadn't? Like every other poor boy in the street, I loved the tales of that famous highwayman. I lurked in the doorways of public houses to listen to his latest exploits, and hid in the shadows of street corners if I ever heard mention of his name, in case there was some new story of his heroics. In my dreams I relived his adventures as he emerged from the forest's edge to waylay another rich man. 'Stand and deliver!' That's what he said to them. 'Your money or your life!' Dick Turpin was my hero.

I was silent for too long, lost in my thoughts.

'Well?' said the captain. 'Have you or haven't you?'

'I have, sir, Captain, sir. I have indeed.'

'Well,' he said, 'I am as sure as I can be that the gentleman who gave you this horse to hold was none other than Dick Turpin himself.'

I stared at the captain in disbelief while a hundred new thoughts charged around my head and got in each other's way.

'And this,' he went on, straightening up and patting the mare's neck, 'is none other than Black Bess.'

CHAPTER EIGHT

I gasped then, out loud. So the mare really was horse royalty. I hadn't tricked those girls at all. In fact, I had undercharged them!

'Black Bess,' I whispered, stroking her nose.

The captain laughed and leaned against her shoulder, one arm thrown loosely over her neck. I have to admit I thought it a cheek for him to take such a liberty with her, as if she was just some old tinker's nag. But he was a captain of the king's guard, so what could I say? And in any event, I very soon forgot about it in the light of what he said next.

'Dick Turpin waylaid and robbed a mail coach and stole a bag of gold coin that was destined for the Bank of England. When he had gone, the driver unhitched the lead horse and rode ahead, where he happened to encounter me and my men while we were on exercise in the countryside. We were able to pick up Turpin's trail while it was still warm, and it led here. His horse's

shoes'– and here he picked up one of Black
Bess's feet so he could show me – 'have
quite an unusual nail pattern, so we had no
difficulty tracking him.'

I nodded glumly, greatly disliking what I
was hearing.

'Perhaps you are mistaken, all the same,
Captain,' I said. 'Perhaps it was some other
man's trail you picked up. I don't think the
man I saw was Dick Turpin.'

He laughed. 'Well, perhaps you're
right,' he said. 'But we shall soon find
out, shan't we? All we need to do is wait
until he returns for his horse, and then
we shall know.'

'And my part in it, Captain?' I said miserably, although I had already guessed.

'Your part is to do exactly what you are doing now. To stand here with Black Bess and wait for her owner to return. Meanwhile my men and I shall be hiding around the area, and when Mr Turpin comes, we shall spring out and arrest him.'

I was mortified, and still trying to get poor Dick Turpin out of this mess. 'Perhaps it won't work, Captain,' I said. 'I've heard it said that Dick Turpin can smell a soldier a mile off by the kind of dubbin you all use on your boots.'

The captain laughed again. 'He will return,' he said, 'because what would Dick Turpin be without Black Bess?' He patted the mare again. 'Where would he find another horse half as fast and as loyal and as brave?'

What was I to do, sir? You can see my predicament. What would you have done? I was so excited, sir, to have met the great Dick Turpin and to be holding his famous horse, but now I was to be bait in a plan to trap him! Worms on a hook, sir, that's what they wanted us to be. Me and poor Black Bess. I looked into her eyes and I knew that she would have hated it as much as me, if only she could understand what was happening.

I thought a lot of thoughts in a very short time, and I'm not proud of all of them. The worst one was about whether

Dick Turpin would have time to hand
me my golden guinea before the soldiers
closed in on him, and the best one had me
dropping Black Bess's reins and walking
away from the whole filthy business.
But there was another one, which lay
somewhere in between, and that was the
one I chose to act upon, and it was this:
as long as I was there holding Black Bess
there was still a chance that Dick Turpin
could get away. If I saw him at a distance,

I might shout out to him and warn him of the trap, and he might be able to run away and hide. And if he just appeared, creeping up out of the alley the way the two thieves had, I might get him to spring up on Black Bess's back and gallop away before the soldiers had time to move in. These chances were slim, I knew, but they were the best I could come up with.

So there was just one small matter that needed to be dealt with.

'What's in it for me, Captain?' I said.

'Dick Turpin promised me a guinea for holding the horse, so I'll be out of pocket, won't I?'

The captain laughed and almost ruffled my hair again, but pulled out at the last minute.

'If we catch Dick Turpin,' he said, 'you will be well rewarded. Have no fear of it.'

He patted the breast of his uniform jacket and I heard the soft music of coinage. And so, although I couldn't do it entirely without shame, I nodded to the captain, and with that nod I agreed to do that piece of work for the King and to play my part in entrapping the man who was my hero and, I liked to think, my friend.

Chapter Nine

The captain and his aide mounted up and went away, leaving the dingy old street empty again. I don't know where they hid their horses, and for that matter, I don't know where they hid themselves. I examined every door and window, every rooftop, every shadow in every alley. But I didn't get one glimpse of a scarlet coat or a dubbined boot.

It had been, to say the least, a very strange day, as I'm sure you understand. I had never in my life been offered so much money by so many people, and yet I still hadn't seen a penny of it. I couldn't decide whether I had made the right decisions, and all the events of the day kept racing round and round in my mind.

Bess wasn't happy, either. She was restless, looking this way and that and tugging on the reins as if she wanted to drag me off along the street. I held on tight and kept her there. I stroked her on the nose to try and calm her, but she shook her head and shoved me so hard in the chest that I nearly fell over.

'There, there, Bess,' I said. 'It's all right.' But she wouldn't look at me now, and I came to believe that she knew exactly what was going on and wanted no part in the unsavoury plan. I kept wishing that I had no part in it, either, sir, but I could not see a way out of it now. I was surrounded by soldiers, and if I tried to run away, I might myself be arrested as a criminal. Several more times Bess pushed me hard with her nose against my chest, and after a while I realized what the problem was. I had lost track of the time we had been standing there together, but it must have been several hours by then, and the poor mare must have been ravenous.

You know something, sir? If I had been
with another lad or girl that day, nothing
could have induced me to share what I
had with them. I had grown up too hard,
I suppose, and when you get as low down
as me, then it's every man for himself,
so to speak. I would have sneaked away
somewhere quiet where I could be on
my own and eat the penny loaf I'd saved
in my pocket, and no one else would have
got so much as a sniff of it.

So why on earth should a horse be any
different? I can't answer that, sir, but I
shared my last bit of bread with that mare
and that is God's honest truth. It didn't
make any sense, either. That loaf was a

meal for me, and it was barely a mouthful
for her, but all the same she had her share,
and more than her share, and despite the
bit in her mouth, she was able to chew it
up and swallow it down, and do you know,
I got nearly as much pleasure from watching
her eat as I did from eating myself.

I'm told the King takes two hours over
his dinner every day, but I can't imagine
that. I never even saw so much food in
one place as would take the King and his
company two hours to eat. I think of that
as heaven. Two hours with nothing else
to do but eat. The mare and I scoffed the
bread in two minutes, sir, or less. And
after that, we were back to the plain old
waiting again.

Kate Thompson

I notice you have a fine pair of boots,
sir, and I doubt you ever knew what it's
like to lose all the feeling in your feet, but
it's a thing I wouldn't wish on my worst
enemy. On the coldest days it happens, and
it's very peculiar. You'd know you were
standing up, but you wouldn't have any
idea what you were standing on. It might
be cobbles and it might be mud and you
might be standing in water up to your
ankles, but unless you took the trouble to
look, you'd have no idea.

And it was beginning to happen to me now, standing there waiting. Usually when it happens, I walk around until my feet warm up or I forget about them, but on this occasion, of course, there was nowhere for me to go. I had no choice but to put up with it.

Dusk began to fall, the grim, early dusk of mid-winter, and the street became busy with people returning from their day's work and setting about their household business. Men and women passed up and down with buckets, on their way to and from the pump. Children were sent out into the street to play while their suppers were cooked, and some of them gathered round to look at Bess. One stupid boy

thought it funny to throw stones at her. I
didn't dare tell him who she belonged to,
but I stopped him by returning one of his
missiles, and hard enough for it to sting.

As dusk gave way to darkness, the
children were sent to round up the pigs
and the chickens, and then everyone
disappeared inside and closed the doors
and the shutters. I don't suppose it was
so warm inside those houses, but from
where I was standing it looked it. The
smells of cooking drove me to distraction.
Candlelight leaked through the door and
window frames, and wood-smoke spilled
from chimneys. It seemed so unfair, sir,
that I had no family to go to and no hearth
to thaw my frozen toes.

I thought about Dick Turpin and
wondered where he was. Somewhere
warm, no doubt. Spending his money
and eating his fill, his high boots
steaming before some
hearty fire.

Highway Robbery

The brief pat and a promise that he had given me began to feel like less of a privilege in the light of that understanding. Perhaps he wasn't such a kind man if he was prepared to leave me in my bare feet in the coming darkness, with the ice on the mud puddles beginning to freeze over again.

Or perhaps it was true, what they said about him. Perhaps he had tried to come and get Black Bess and give me my guinea, but he'd got a whiff of the dubbin on the soldiers' boots and had turned away, smelling the trap we had laid for him.

I was looking at a long night ahead of me in the bitter cold, and I began to wish that it had never been my misfortune to meet Dick Turpin and Black Bess.

CHAPTER TEN

They came in the night, sir, as I might have guessed they would, Toothless and his portly friend.

I never saw or heard them coming at all. They just appeared, sneaking silently up the alley behind me.

My first thought when I saw them was to take their thirty shillings and run. Even if the soldiers caught me, I'd be better off than I would standing there and perishing in the cold. But they never offered it this time. They just pushed me into the mud and made off with the horse.

I'm not very big, sir, as you can see, but I can make a big noise if I choose to, and I did so then. The door of the nearest house opened, but I was already running after the men and Black Bess. I needn't have, though. Because the soldiers had also appeared, as if from nowhere, and they were everywhere around us in the dark, blocking every mouth of every alley. The men tried to make a run for it, but they hadn't a hope.

They were collared in no time and brought back to my corner, and pushed against the wall. There was plenty of light by this time, because the commotion had caused half the people in the street to open their doors. And the other half, I suppose, to bolt them more securely.

'But the horse is mine,' Mudbreeks was saying. 'That urchin stole her from me.'

'Is that true, lad?' said the captain, strolling in from one of the alleyways. 'Is this the man who asked you to look after his horse?'

I'm good at thinking on my feet, sir. You have to be if you live on your wits, like I do. But on that occasion I didn't think fast enough. It could all have been over, you

see. If I had said yes, there could have been
an end to it all.

'But he promised me a guinea and now
he has to give it to me' is what I should
have said. Muddybreeks would gladly have
given me a guinea to get off the hook, and
he would have got himself a great bargain.
As for me, I could have taken myself off
to the nearest pie shop and got myself a
bellyful of steak and kidney.

But there was an even better outcome
to that particular plan, and it was this. If
I named Muddybreeks as the owner of
the horse, then the soldiers would stop
watching for Dick Turpin, wouldn't they?
So when he did come back for Black Bess,
he would be disappointed, of course, and

he would think that I had let him down,
and that would be very unfortunate if it
were to happen that I encountered him
again some day. But what matters is that
he would have his freedom, and he could
go about his business on the highways.
It was, in fact, the perfect solution to
everyone's problems.

But did I say *yes*?

No. I said *no*.

Two such small words, sir, but what a
big difference between them. I said no,
and the soldiers laid hands on the two
men instantly, as if they were following
my personal orders. Such a sense of power
that gave me, but it didn't last for long.
Muddybreeches spat at me as they took

him away, which goes to prove that he
was no gentleman, despite his waistcoat
and his boots.

Three of the soldiers went with the men and the rest vanished back to wherever they had been hiding before. Only the captain remained behind, and he clapped me on the shoulder and said:

'Back to your post, young man.'

My heart sank at the thought of more standing around in the darkness and the cold. But what could I do? I led the mare back to our station and adjusted the cloak on her back. It was wonderfully warm beneath it, where the heavy woollen cloth trapped the heat from her body, and I envied her and wondered how it was that a beast could be so well provided for and comfortable when I was so miserable and cold. But that was my lot, sir, and I was

well accustomed to suffering it, so I pulled
my tattered old coat round me as tight as
I could and stamped my icy feet up and
down on the ground.

I don't know how long we stood like
that, with the mare moving her weight
from one hind leg to the other and myself
leaning against the wall and doing the
same thing. I know there are some people
who take pleasure from the hours of
darkness, but I'm not one of them. It's
during the night that I remember my life
at home before my mother died, and when
there is nothing to look at, it's difficult
to keep your mind away from dwelling
on the bad things that happen. I measure
my days by the passage of the sun through

the sky and by the length of the roads
and streets I travel, but I have no way of
measuring the hours of darkness, so I
have no idea what time of night it was
when Black Bess grew tired of standing
and, very carefully, laid herself down on
her belly.

And now that she no longer towered
over me, I saw a way in which we could
share Dick Turpin's cloak and both stay
warm beneath it. I had never sat astride a
horse before, but with her back now so
close to the ground, it didn't seem to me to
be a very great risk to take when the return
was the promise of such warmth.

Very slowly and quietly, taking care
not to alarm the mare, I put the reins back
over her head and climbed into the saddle.
She sighed in the darkness but she made
no other objection. I pushed myself to
the very back of the saddle, then leaned
forward over her withers. The cloak came
over my back and up to my neck, but a
draught still came in beneath it, so I felt

along the collar until I found the buckle
and strap, and I fastened them beneath
my chin.

The cloth still held a rank smell from
the mare's dried sweat, but it held the
heat from her body as well, and I began
to warm up so fast that I got pains in my
hands and feet. But there was pleasure too,
sir: the pure delight of being warm, and
even before the pains had faded away I
had drifted off into sleep, with my cheek
resting on the mare's thick mane.

CHAPTER ELEVEN

I woke to the alarming sensation of the mare clambering to her feet beneath me. It was so dark that I thought my eyes were gummed together, as they often are when I wake up in the mornings, but then I caught a glimpse of a few stars above the rooftops and I knew it was still the dead of night.

'Off you get, lad. It's all up.'

It was the captain's voice, and now I could make out his form in the street beside me. But I was looking down at him instead of up, because I was sitting up high on the mare's back.

'What's all up?' I said. 'What's happening?'

'Two constables caught Dick Turpin yesterday afternoon. The report of it has only just reached us.'

He sounded very cross. I wondered whose fault it was that he and his men had stood for half the night in the freezing cold, waiting to catch a man who had already been caught.

'So down you get, and off home with you.'

But I wasn't ready to get down, and in any case I had no home to go to. And there was another thing.

'What about my payment?' I said.

'Oh, hang your payment,' said the captain, and he reached up to take hold of my arm and pull me down.

But I wasn't coming down. My heart
filled with fury at the way I had been used.
Did he really think that he could treat me
like that? Keep me standing around all day
and night and then just send me on
my way without so much as a
sixpence? I yanked my arm
away and kicked out at
him as hard as I could.
I missed him by a
mile, but as my leg
returned, my heel
slammed hard
into Black Bess's
flank. And,
noblest of mares,
she didn't need to

be asked twice. She spun away from my heel and lit out along the street as though the devil was after her. Lord knows how I stayed in the saddle, but now that we were moving I clung on to her mane as tight as I could, knowing that my life might very well depend upon it.

It's a good thing that horses see better in the dark than people do, because I had no idea where we were going. Black Bess did, though, and her feet were sure and safe as she splashed through the muck and ice. Soon I could tell by the smell of the air that we had left the city behind and entered the countryside beyond. Still the mare galloped on, showing no sign of tiring. I very much wished she would.

I had no idea whether the soldiers
were in pursuit, but I had another serious
problem which might prove even more
dangerous to me than them. The cloak,
Dick Turpin's wonderful warm black
cloak, was streaming out behind me just
as it had streamed behind him when he
galloped into town the previous day.

How he arranged it I have no idea, but I
am sure it wasn't throttling him the way it
was now throttling me. And because I was
no rider I didn't dare lift a hand from my
grip on the mare's mane in case I tumbled
off the side on to the unseen road rushing
past beneath us. The reins were there
somewhere, flapping against her neck and
the backs of my hands, but it was going to

require a huge leap of faith for me to try
and grab them.

Unless I did, though, I would be
strangled by Dick Turpin's cloak, and it
seemed like a particularly stupid way to
die, given all that I had gone through.
So I took one hand from Black Bess's
mane and groped about in the wind that
was whistling past her neck, until I felt
the cold, greasy leather of the rein, and
clutched at it.

Being a rider yourself, sir – and a fine
one, I dare say – you will know better
than to haul on one rein while leaving the
other to dangle free. Had I been stronger
it is likely that I would have brought
Black Bess down, and myself along with

her in a heap in the mud. But as it was
I only succeeded in turning her off the
road and into a grove of trees, where she
was obliged to come to a very rapid stop.
Naturally I went straight over her head and
landed in a bramble patch, with the black
cloak settling on top of me.

Highway Robbery

And I was still trying to disentangle myself from that muddle when I heard the thunder of hooves on the road behind us, as the king's captain and his troop of soldiers went flying past.

Yet again trying to capture someone who wasn't there.

Chapter Twelve

So that's my story, sir. And I don't know how you would feel about it, but it seems to me that the mare is rightfully mine. She was left in my care, you see, and the man who owned her is due to be hanged very shortly,

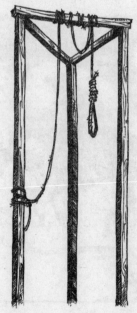

as I'm sure you will have heard, and he has
no use for her now.

It did cross my mind to take up where
Dick Turpin left off, and to pursue the
highwayman's trade. But I'm small, sir, as
you can see, and I can't imagine coachmen
or travellers paying much attention to
me, especially since Dick Turpin took his
saddlebag with him and left me with no
pistol.

So that's why I'm offering her for sale,
sir, because I'm a poor city lad and can't
afford to keep a horse. The cloak too, if
you were interested, though it wouldn't
come cheap because of its fascinating
history.

Yes, I've heard the same thing myself,
sir; that there are other people out there
claiming to be in possession of Black Bess
and offering her for sale. All I can say to

that is: see for yourself. You don't need
me to point out what a fine animal you're
looking at.

Well, naturally she looks a bit tired.
Wouldn't you, sir, if you'd been through
what she has? And of course a new set
of shoes would make her feet look a lot
tidier. Well, maybe she could use a bit of
a trim around the fetlocks, but really, sir,
to call her a carthorse is most unfair.

No, no. I couldn't take that for her.
That's an insult. She's worth ten times
that. This is Black Bess you're looking at,
sir, not just any old nag.

I see. Well, suit yourself, sir. No charge
for looking. And there are plenty more
horsemen out there that will leap at the

chance of buying the one and only
Black Bess. I'll have no trouble selling
her, will I, Bess? No trouble at all.

THE END

Kate Thompson is a born storyteller and a uniquely imaginative and thought-provoking writer. *The New Policeman* won both the Whitbread Children's Book Award and the Guardian Children's Fiction Prize in 2005, and the inaugural Irish BA Award for Children's Books in 2006. Kate Thompson is also three times winner of the Irish Children's Book of the Year Bisto Award for *The Beguilers* (2002), *The Alchemist's Apprentice* (2003) and *Annan Water* (2005).

She has trained racehorses, travelled extensively in India, working and learning, and writes poetry as well as novels. Over the last few years she has developed a passion for playing the fiddle and has completed an MA in Traditional Irish Music Performance.

Kate Thompson lives on the west coast of Ireland.